The OWL
and the
PUSSY-CAT

* *For Emma* *
♥

THE OWL AND THE PUSSY-CAT
A DOUBLEDAY BOOK: 0 385 405707
A PICTURE CORGI BOOK: 0 552 528196

First published in Great Britain by Doubleday

PRINTING HISTORY
Doubleday edition published 1995
Picture Corgi edition published 1996

Doubleday and Picture Corgi Books are published by
Transworld Publishers Ltd,
61-63 Uxbridge Road, Ealing, London W5 5SA,
in Australia by Transworld Publishers (Australia) Pty. Ltd,
15-25 Helles Avenue, Moorebank, NSW 2170,
and in New Zealand by Transworld Publishers (NZ) Ltd,

3 William Pickering Drive, Albany, Auckland.

Made and printed in Belgium by Proost

The

OWL
and the
PUSSY-CAT

EDWARD LEAR

Illustrated by
IAN BECK

DOUBLEDAY/PICTURE CORGI BOOKS.

The Owl and the Pussy-cat went to sea

In a beautiful pea-green boat,

They took some honey,

and plenty of money,

Wrapped up in a five-pound note.

The Owl looked up to the stars above,
And sang to a small guitar,

"O lovely Pussy! O Pussy my love,
What a beautiful Pussy you are,
You are,
You are!
What a beautiful Pussy you are!"

Pussy said to the Owl, "You elegant fowl!
How charmingly sweet you sing!

O let us be married! Too long we have tarried:
But what shall we do for a ring?"

January

February

May

June

September

October

They sailed away, for a year and a day

march

April

July

August

November

December

And there in a wood a Piggy-wig stood

With a ring at the end of his nose,
His nose,
His nose,
With a ring at the end of his nose.

"Dear Pig, are you willing to sell for one shilling

Your ring?" Said the Piggy, "I will."

So they took it away, and were married next day

By the Turkey who lives on the hill.

They dined on mince,

and slices of quince,

Which they ate with a runcible spoon;

And hand in hand, on the edge of the sand,

They danced by the light of the moon,

The moon,
The moon,

They danced by the light of the moon.

Also by Ian Beck,
and published by Doubleday/Picture Corgi Books:

THE TEDDY ROBBER

HUSH-A-BYE BABY

EMILY AND THE GOLDEN ACORN

TOM AND THE ISLAND OF DINOSAURS

PETER & THE WOLF

Accompanying audio cassettes:

HUSH-A-BYE BABY

PETER & THE WOLF

THE OWL AND THE PUSSY-CAT
AND OTHER ANIMAL SONGS